I Can Tell Time

At the Beach
The Parts of a Day

by Alice Proctor

MEDINAH PRIMARY SCHOOL
22W300 SUNNYSIDE ROAD
MEDINAH, IL 60157

WEEKLY READER PUBLISHING

Math and Curriculum Consultant:
Debra Voege, M.A.,
Science and Math Curriculum Resource Teacher

Please visit our web site at: www.garethstevens.com
For a free color catalog describing our list of high-quality books,
call 1-800-542-2595 (USA) or 1-800-387-3178 (Canada).

Library of Congress Cataloging-in-Publication Data

Proctor, Alice, 1967-
    At the beach: the parts of a day / Alice Proctor.
        p. cm. — (I can tell time)
      ISBN-10: 0-8368-8388-8 — ISBN-13: 978-0-8368-8388-6 (lib. bdg.)
      ISBN-10: 0-8368-8393-4 — ISBN-13: 978-0-8368-8393-0 (softcover)
      1. Time—Juvenile literature.   2. Days—Juvenile literature.
3. Beaches—Juvenile literature. I. Title.
    QB209.5.P76   2007
    529'.7—dc22   2007017436

This North American edition first published in 2008 by
Weekly Reader® Books
An imprint of Gareth Stevens Publishing
1 Reader's Digest Road
Pleasantville, NY 10570-7000 USA

This U.S. edition copyright © 2008 by Gareth Stevens, Inc. Original
edition copyright © 2007 by ticktock Entertainment Ltd. First published
in Great Britain in 2007 by ticktock Media Ltd., Unit 2, Orchard Business
Centre, North Farm Road, Tunbridge Wells, Kent, TN2 3XF, United Kingdom.

Gareth Stevens series editor: Dorothy L. Gibbs
Gareth Stevens graphic design and cover design: Dave Kowalski
Gareth Stevens art direction: Tammy West

Picture credits: (t=top, b=bottom, c=center, l=left, r=right)
Alamy: 7 both, 10r, 23l, 24tl. Getty Images/National Geographic: 19b.
Image Source: 1, 8, 9t, 11, 13, 14, 15 main. Jupiter Images/Image 100:
cover. Photolibrary: 18t. Shutterstock: 5 both, 8-9 background, 10l, 12 all,
15l, 16, 17bl, 21 all, 23 cl, cr, r, 24 tr, bl, br. Superstock: 4, 6, 17tr, 18b.
Ticktock Media Archive: 20.

Every effort has been made to trace the copyright holders for the pictures used in this
book. We apologize in advance for any unintentional omissions and would be
pleased to insert the appropriate acknowledgements in any subsequent edition.

Printed in the United States of America

1 2 3 4 5 6 7 8 9 11 10 09 08 07

Contents

Glossary words are printed in **boldface** type in the text.

All in a Day

We are going to the beach. We will be there all day. A day is a long time. Here are some things I spend time doing each day.

Time to Eat

Breakfast

A **day** starts in the **morning**. I eat breakfast in the morning.

Lunch

The middle of the day is called **noon**. Lunchtime is at noon. The time after lunch is called the **afternoon**.

Dinner

At the end of the afternoon, I eat dinner. Dinner is my last big meal of the day.

Time to Play

I get home from school in the afternoon. Then it is time to play. I like to build things with my wooden blocks. On the **weekend**, I can play all day!

Time to Sleep

In the **evening**, it starts getting dark outside. It is almost **night**. I go to bed in the evening and sleep through the night.

How do you spend the time in a day?

My Day at the Beach

I wake up early in the morning. Outside, the Sun is coming up. It is going to be a warm, sunny day.

Time for Breakfast

I eat cereal for breakfast. I eat an apple, too.

Breakfast gives me energy to start the day. I will need lots of energy at the beach!

Time to Go

I help Mom pack everything we need for swimming and playing at the beach. Mom says, "Don't forget to pack some sunscreen."

I help Dad load everything into the car. Now we are ready to go to the beach!

What do you take to the beach?

Morning at the Beach

I can't wait to get to the beach. We have been driving for a long time. Mom keeps telling us we're almost there.

We're here!

We can smell the ocean, and we hear the waves crashing. The Sun is higher in the sky now, and the air is getting very warm. We all want to go swimming.

Mom helps my little sister put on some sunscreen. My brother and I put on our own sunscreen.

Time for a Swim

We run into the water. Mom and Dad come, too. The water is cold. It makes my skin tingle.

We have a great time splashing around in the ocean. After we swim, we fly our kite on the beach.

Have you ever gone swimming in the ocean?

Noon at the Beach

Now the Sun is very high. It is right above us! Dad says he feels hungry.

Time for Lunch

Dad shows us his watch. We see that both hands on the watch are pointing at the 12.

Dad tells us the time. It is 12 **o'clock** noon. Mom says it is time to eat our sandwiches.

After Lunch

After we eat our sandwiches, my sister and I play in the sand. We build a really big sandcastle. Dad says that, in one **hour**, we will all go exploring.

Before we go, we put on more sunscreen and have a cool drink of water.

Drinking a lot of water is important on hot days.

11

Afternoon at the Beach

It is 2 o'clock in the afternoon. We still have a lot of time left for exploring.

Time to Look Around

There are so many things to see on the beach. We spend a long time looking at shells.

A hermit crab has a spiral shell.

A clam shell opens and closes like a mouth.

As we explore, we leave everything where we find it.

Time for a Game

The Sun is not right above us anymore, but the air is still warm.

We brought along our racquets to play beach tennis. Dad and I play against Mom and my brother. Yippee! Dad and I win two games.

What games do you like to play at the beach?

Time to Go Home

The Sun is getting lower in the sky, and the air is feeling cooler. Soon it will be time to go home.

One Last Swim

Mom says we have time for one more swim.

We race to the water. The water feels much warmer now than it did this morning.

Swimming in the ocean is so much fun!

Time to Pack Up

Dad says it is 4 o'clock now. We have to pack up everything and load it all back into the car. We also have to make sure we do not leave any litter on the beach.

We are all very tired. We are getting hungry, too. We have had a busy day.

Do you always clean up your litter?

At Home in the Evening

By the time we get home, we are very hungry! Mom starts making dinner, but she says we can't eat until we are clean!

Time to Wash Up

Look at my feet! The sand has stuck to the sunscreen. I even have sand between my toes! It is time for me to take a shower.

Dinnertime

Fish and yummy vegetables is a good meal after a day at the beach. While we eat dinner, we talk about how much fun we had swimming and exploring.

After dinner, I look across the field behind our house. The Sun is going down, and the sky is starting to get dark. Dad says this time of day is called **dusk**.

Dusk is during the evening part of a day.

Nighttime

The Sun has set. The Moon is out, and stars are twinkling. It is night now.

Time for Bed

After dinner, my sister and I play games for a while. Then it is time to get ready for bed.

We brush our teeth and put on our pajamas. My sister goes to bed first. I am older than my sister so my bedtime is 30 **minutes** later than hers.

Find It at the BEACH

Find It on a CORAL REEF

Story Time

Before I go to sleep, my Dad reads to me. Tonight, he reads my favorite books about the beach and the ocean.

Time to Dream

I wonder what I will dream about after a day at the beach. Maybe I will dream about building a sandcastle as big as a house!

What do you dream about at the end of a fun day?

Time Facts

There are lots of things to learn about time. How many of these facts do you know?

Days and Weeks

Days of the Week
There are seven days in a **week**.

Monday
Tuesday
Wednesday
Thursday
Friday
Saturday
Sunday

Hours in a Day
Each day lasts 24 hours and has daytime and nighttime.

The parts of a day are morning, noon, afternoon, evening, and night.

Telling Time
People use clocks and watches to tell the time of the day.

Months and Years

Which month is your birthday in?

Months of the Year

A **year** has 12 months.

January

February

March

April

May

June

July

August

September

October

November

December

spring

summer

autumn

winter

Seasons

A year also has four seasons. The seasons are spring, summer, autumn, and winter.

What season is it now?

Times to Remember

You have learned lots of exciting things about time in this book. How many do you remember?

Put the words in each of the boxes below in the correct order.

Saturday
Monday   Friday
Thursday
Sunday   Wednesday
Tuesday

December
July   May   April
August   November
June
January   October
March
September   February

noon   night
afternoon
evening   morning

What part of the day is it?

Match each part of the day with the right picture.

| evening | morning | night | noon |

What part of the day is it now?

Glossary

afternoon – the part of a day between 12 o'clock noon and the time when the Sun starts to set

day – a period of time that starts and ends at 12 o'clock midnight and lasts 24 hours

dusk – a time in the evening, when daylight is becoming dim

evening – the part of a day between afternoon and night, when the Sun is setting

hour – a measure of time that equals 60 minutes. Each day has 24 hours.

minutes – measures of time that equal 60 seconds. Each hour has 60 minutes.

morning – the part of a day between 12 o'clock midnight and 12 o'clock noon

night – the part of a day when it is dark outside and when most people sleep

noon – the 12 o'clock hour in the middle of the day

o'clock – any hour of the day when the big hand on a clock is pointing exactly at the 12. The little hand shows what hour it is.

week – a measure of time that equals 7 days

weekend – the two days at the end of a week, which are Saturday and Sunday

year – a measure of time that has 12 months and 4 seasons. Each month is made up of approximately 4 weeks, and each week has 7 days.

Answers

Monday	Friday	morning	January	July
Tuesday	Saturday	noon	February	August
Wednesday	Sunday	afternoon	March	September
Thursday		evening	April	October
		night	May	November
			June	December

morning   noon

evening   night